MINEFIELDS AND MINISKIRTS

Australian Women and the Vietnam War

Adapted by Terence O'Connell from Siobhán McHugh's book

CURRENCY PRESS
The performing arts publisher

First published in 2004
by Currency Press Pty Ltd,
Gadigal Land, PO Box 2287, Strawberry Hills, NSW, 2012, Australia
enquiries@currency.com.au
www.currency.com.au
in association with Playbox Theatre Melbourne.

This revised edition published in 2005.

Reprinted 2011, 2019 (twice), 2020, 2022, 2023

Typeset by Dean Nottle for Currency Press.
Printed by Fineline Print + Copy Services, Revesby, NSW.

A catalogue record for this book is available from the National Library of Australia

Contents

Terence O'Connell dedicates the play to all the Australian women involved with the Vietnam War and to the wives and families of all Vietnam Veterans.

Minefileds and Miniskirts was first produced by Playbox Theatre, at The C.U.B.Malthouse, Melbourne, on 14 July 2004 with the following cast:

THE VOLUNTEER	Robyn Arthur
THE JOURNALIST	Tracy Bartram
THE NURSE	Debra Byrne
THE VET'S WIFE	Tracy Mann
THE ENTERTAINER	Wendy Stapleton

Director, Terence O'Connell
Designer, Catherine Raven
Lighting Designer, Phil Lethlean
Sound Designer, Rod Davies
Director's Associate, Ken Moffat
Choreographer, Alana Scanlan

ACKNOWLEDGEMENTS

'Leaving on a Jet Plane' (John Denver)
Lyrics reprinted by permission of Essex Music of Australia Pty. Ltd.

'The Circle Game' (Joni Mitchell)
Lyrics reprinted by permission of Essex Music of Australia Pty. Ltd.

'One Tin Soldier' (Dennis Lambert/Brian Potter)
Lyrics reprinted by permission of Universal/MCA Music Publishing Pty. Ltd.

'Saigon Bride' (Joan Baez/Nina Dusheck)
Lyrics reprinted by permission of Cromwell Music Australia Pty. Ltd. and Warner/Chappell Music Australia, Pty Ltd. © Belwin/CCP Inc.

CHARACTERS

MARGARET, the Vet's wife
SANDY, the entertainer
KATHY, the nurse
EVE, the volunteer
RUTH, the journalist

The pre-show music is themes from Vietnam War era movies.

As the audience enters, they see a silk curtain. Written on it, in bleached-out handwriting, is the following: 'During the 1960s and early 1970s, close to a thousand Australian women were in wartime Vietnam. Nurses, entertainers, secretaries, volunteers and consular staff. Though their backgrounds varied as much as their experiences, they have one thing in common. Vietnam transformed their lives and haunted their memories...'

SCENE ONE: PROLOGUE

MARGARET *appears in front of the curtain. She is dressed for a wintry day in the 1980s.*

In the distance, military drums are heard and 'The Colonel Bogie March' plays.

MARGARET: I never came to the March, or hadn't for a few years, but I saw on the news that the women who'd been in the war were marching for the first time, so I thought I'd go. I hadn't been there, to that war, in a country on the South China Sea. I hadn't been out of Australia. But I'd been married to a Vet, so I felt like I'd had my own Vietnam. And I was watching these women grouping up before the March. And the conversation was quite loud and I felt like I wanted to go up to them and talk too.

The silk curtain is lit from behind and we see the silhouettes of four women as they speak.

SANDY: Helicopters took us up to a bald hill. There was a steel girder, a generator and a tent. While the boys in the band set up the equipment, we got in the tent, got dressed, painted on the glamour. The band started playing 'Proud Mary', and when we came out, go-going in our pink feathers, there were thousands of screaming GIs on tanks and trucks and the bald hill was covered with a mass of men in uniform. They said that we stopped the war, that even the Viet Cong were watching at the bottom of the hill in the trees.

KATHY: The Americans would invite us to a dance and then build a dance-floor for us! We were 'round eyes' as they called us. They'd send a chopper and we'd be drinking champagne flying up-country to a party. And while you were jiving away to the sound of falling rockets, you'd mention casually that we were short of blood at the hospital. And as that chopper flew you home, you'd be thinking of the hundred GIs who'd be lined up the next morning, ready to give blood. And they'd be armed with cigarettes, chewing gum and Hershey Bars. Bloody bliss.

EVE: Up in a helicopter, I watched a firefight across a paddy field. The choppers hovering above and there's this old man with his water buffalo, ploughing his rice paddy. As if it wasn't happening. It's all going on just above his head, the tracers flying through the air, explosions everywhere. And he's working on, keeping on going, even the buffalo wasn't letting all this carnage stop them ploughing the rice. As they must have done forever. And somehow, I knew this war would never be 'won', that they had the history of the ages on their side.

RUTH: I was there. I was so young. And it was wondrous, like a big Luna Park every day of the week. Let's try a new ride. Let's jump out of a chopper and walk through a paddy field. I was traveling in a jeep with two American soldiers when we came under heavy fire. We were three people up against what we thought was a batallion and we were convinced we were all going to die anyway. We dived for cover and a soldier tossed me an M16. I said, 'I don't know how to fire this!' And he said, 'Just pull the goddamn trigger, ma'am'.

They all talk in a babble as they repeat their opening speeches. The sound of helicopters. They stop instantly.

MARGARET: And I worked up the courage and went to cross the road to speak to them, but as I did there was a ceremonial fly-over of helicopters above us. The talk stopped instantly. You could have heard a pin drop, apart from the whirr of the choppers above us. All those women were lost in their déjà vu and I was lost in it with them…

The silhouettes disappear, the helicopters get louder and then are replaced by the major musical theme.

As she exits, MARGARET *pulls back the silk curtain. It reveals a 'french colonial' wrought-iron gate, flanked by silk prayer ribbons. A bamboo and wooden-slatted set. An aged, planked floor on stilts floating above a lush, green paddy field.*

There are five chairs, five small tables and a small bar. The style of the furniture ranges from beautiful, classic Vietnamese pieces through to red plastic 'Coca Cola' street furniture. Vietnamese silk and basket lanterns hang over the set and out into the auditorium. Bamboo 'legs' at the side of the set feature aged, watermarked portraits of the women, as they were in Vietnam thirty years ago. Props such as fans, umbrellas, zippo lighters and teacups will be used.

SCENE TWO: OFF TO WAR

One by one, the five characters enter through the wrought-iron gate. They wear Vietnamese-inspired clothing, pants and tunics, in deep, rich colours. Each of their jackets is embroidered with a different Australian 'symbol'. They all carry small suitcases. They speak directly to the audience.

SANDY: You could find me any Saturday evening at a surburban club, in my miniskirt and Carnaby Street cap, sweet sixteen, up on a tacky stage belting out 'These Boots Are Made For Walking'. And I was dying to walk, too, out of the dreary place I lived in, with its rows of broken-down, grey terrace houses and blood-house pubs. The only bit of colour was the Chinese restaurant where we'd queue with our saucepans for sweet and sour on Friday nights. My mum scraped together money each week for singing lessons for me and took us to all the Hollywood musicals. She loved 'With a Song In My Heart', Susan Hayward entertaining the American troops, we'd go whenever it was on. Maybe that movie planted the idea in me. Anyway, on this particular Saturday night, and I'll never forget it, I won second prize in a talent quest; the meat tray. The girl who won asked me to join a trio, The Velveteens, who were going to Vietnam as part of a concert party to entertain the American troops. Mum loved the idea,

Dad had been gone for years and there was no other way of me having an adventure, so of course I said yes.

'LEAVING ON A JET PLANE' (Peter, Paul & Mary)

SANDY: [*singing*]

All my bags are packed, I'm ready to go
I'm standing here outside your door
I hate to wake you up to say goodbye
But the dawn is breakin', it's early morn
The taxi's waiting, he's blowin' his horn
Already I'm so lonesome I could cry…

EVE: It was a Saturday. We lived in the big house next to the Church of England in a leafy suburb. My father was the Minister. My mother ran the Ladies' Church Auxiliary and I learnt about serving others from them. I'd had my time of rebellion, of fluffy ducks and discoteques, marijuana and midnight swims, but I'd returned to the fold. Even though I was still searching for some sort of freedom, some mad idea of a 'Girls' Own' adventure. Here I was, in the kitchen with my mother, helping ice the cake for my wedding to a really nice boy from the Church Fellowship. On the wireless was an interview with someone from the World Council of Churches, talking about how they were looking for volunteers to go to Vietnam. I said, 'I'm so sorry, Mum, but I can't get married now'. I was already imagining myself with my Pan Am cabin bag, winging my way to Saigon…

SANDY & EVE: [*together, singing*]

There's so many times I've let you down
So many times I've played around
I tell you now, they don't mean a thing
Every place I go, I think of you
Every song I sing, I sing for you
When I come back, I'll wear your wedding ring…

KATHY: I lived with my dad in a country town. He'd been a POW on the Burma Railway, and his father had been a soldier and his father before him. I was a nurse and when I heard nurses were needed, I wanted to carry on the family tradition, so I applied to go. There was a chart in the kitchen, a map on the wall, with all these yellow eyes looking down on Australia. 'The Yellow Peril, love.' But I only went there to look after our boys. Just like in the storybooks, although it didn't end like the storybooks. I was in the staff room on a Saturday night, watching the ABC news, and they were reading out the names of the nurses going to Vietnam on bloody national television. My name was the last and I raced down to check with Matron. And she said, 'Yes, Kath, you are going, but don't tell anyone, dear, it's a secret'. Within days we were flown out, first class, gearing up for war on strawberries and champagne. It was the first time I'd ever been on a plane.

SANDY, EVE & KATHY: [*together, singing*]

So kiss me and smile for me
Tell me that you'll wait for me
Hold me like you'll never let me go
I'm leavin' on a jet plane
Don't know when I'll be back again…

RUTH: I was a journalist locked in the tabloid world of the 'Women's Pages', the Miss Australia Quest, Ladies Day at the Races and fondue parties. I was in a pub in Flinders Street drinking with some journos, for a change, and complaining about my lot and how it was driving me crazy. I wanted to escape. They were all bored shitless with this, they heard it every Friday night after I'd had a few. And someone said if I seriously wanted an adventure I should get myself accredited to write in Vietnam. He actually said, 'Go on, Ruth, I dare you!' And I said, 'You're on!' A few weeks later, on a Saturday morning, a messenger from the wire service arrived, with a one-way ticket to Saigon…

SANDY, EVE, KATHY & RUTH: [*together, singing*]

Now the time has come to leave you
One more time, let me kiss you
Then close your eyes, I'll be on my way
Dream about the days to come
When I won't have to leave alone
About the times I won't have to say…

MARGARET: Saturday nights I'd be dressed to the nines for Ballroom Dancing at the local Town Hall. Too much make-up and hairspray, but, at nineteen, I thought I looked fabulous. Mambo, cha-cha, tango, waltz, I could do them all. With style. I was a young girl having fun and the Vietnam War was a world away to me. I couldn't have found that place on a map if you paid me. I was attempting to glide around the floor with a sweaty bloke who was treading all over my toes and holding me a bit too tight, when I noticed a handsome boy looking shy in a corner. That was it. I fell in love instantly. He looked at me and of course I didn't know then that the glance between us would link me with the Vietnam War forever…

ALL: [*together, singing*]

So kiss me and smile for me
Tell me that you'll wait for me
Hold me like you'll never let me go
I'm leaving on a jet plane
I don't know when I'll be back again
I don't know when I'll be back again
I don't know when I'll be back again.

A round robin tail-out of the chorus. They wave, then freeze in a tableau of youthful adventure.

SCENE THREE: HELLO VIETNAM

We hear the sounds of a busy, chaotic, wartime Saigon.

MARGARET: And we were married. At the Registry Office.

SANDY *stands beside* MARGARET *and flicks open a fan, revealing the face of a young soldier.*

He looked so handsome in his uniform, even allowing for the bad army haircut. We had our honeymoon, three days in Coolangatta at the Golden Sands Motel. We were never up early enough for the 'Complimentary Continental Breakfast'. We kissed in the surf, like Deborah Kerr and Burt Lancaster in *From Here To Eternity*. We walked along the beach at night, arm in arm, in love with our love and dreaming of our future. On his last night home we had a farewell waltz at the Town Hall and the next morning I waved him goodbye and started to cry. He said, 'Oh, come on, darling, kiss me, smile for me, I'll be fine. I'm bloody invincable!' I went to live in the army quarters, with a prison farm on one side and a mental institution on the other. Handy! There were bloody prowlers every night. So I'd wash his clothes and hang them out every week so it'd look like he was home.

The 'Saigon' musical theme is heard underneath the following.

RUTH: I arrived at my new home, the Hotel Nautique, on a street of Hondas, hawkers and hookers, when I'd been expecting something a bit more Graham Greene. I walked into the foyer and the bar girls hated me on sight.

EVE, KATHY *and* SANDY *flick open fans showing the faces of three bar girls.*

They drank crème de menthe, smoked Salem cigarettes and glared at me. They thought I was there to take some of their trade. When I told them I was a journalist, they started to laugh and talk. And given the bloody sanitised version of things I'd get from the American press machine, those girls became my best contacts for what was really going on. I became very adept at throwing back those crème de menthes and doing the drawback on a Salem. For professional reasons only. I was about to experience the thrill of being on the bayonet border of the world.

EVE: I came out of the airport, got into a cyclo and was whirled into that incredible traffic.

SANDY, KATHY *and* RUTH *create a moving cyclo with umbrellas and a small table.* EVE *steps inside it.*

A surging sea of motorbikes, bicycles and broken-down cars where there appeared to be no road rules at all. The noise was deafening, the filth, the smell, people peeing in the street! I thought I saw bloodstains everywhere, but it turned out it was the juice of the betel nut that they'd spit out on the footpaths. Then I was in my miserable little hotel room, having a bit of a cry, wondering what I'd got myself into. I was sitting on the toilet and next to me was another toilet, a funny shape. I fiddled around with the knobs and suddenly this fountain sprung up. I thought maybe it was a baby bath so put my aching feet into it. I'd never seen a bidet before! A week later I was washing my smalls in it. But I pulled myself together, said a prayer, put on a brave face and walked out into my new world. Alleyways with stall after stall of fabulously-coloured Thai silks, markets with vats of twitching eels, buckets of live frogs, piles of pigs' ears and snouts. Beautiful, young bar girls and drunken soldiers spilling out of nightclubs. I walked past Uncle Sam's Bar 'n' Grill. I turned a corner into Tu Do, and there were little children, all with their hands blown off, begging. Saigon was a street of walking wounded and I thought then, I'll do my best for these poor children if it's the last thing I ever do.

KATHY: Deep in the Mekong Delta, I arrived at the hospital site and the first thing I saw was a dog, on a rubbish dump, eating a human leg.

The women sweep the area with straw brooms, polish the furniture, etc.

There was no water, no electricity, no equipment, no instruments, no mattresses. We spent the first week cleaning, scrubbing, painting. In the beginning we lived in the red dirt with bum-hole toilets. My dad was a plumber and he was furious when I wrote to him. Especially seeing the Yanks had hot showers and flush toilets. He caused a bit of a stir with his Member of Parliament and soon after two bathtubs arrived. But we didn't have plumbing, so we sent one to the hospital and kept the other one for party nights when we'd fill it with ice, Coca Cola and bloody Four X beer.

SANDY: Straight away, we were doing three shows a day on stages ranging from the back of a truck to a pontoon on the Mekong Delta. Our approval write-up said: 'An all-singing, dancing floorshow composed of four lovely females and three males. All females do solo dances, fine music accompaniment due to an excellent drummer and an echo chamber. A real GI crowd-pleaser'. The second show we ever did we heard an explosion and hit the deck in our showgirl feathers. And when we looked up, a GI tripping on acid had thrown a grenade. The first few rows were full of seriously wounded soldiers, when seconds before they'd been smiling, cheering boys. As the medics rushed in to stretcher them away, a colonel said, 'Sing a hymn for them, girls'.

[*Singing*] Amazing grace how sweet the sound…

The women flick on zippo lighters that flicker as they sing.

ALL: [*together, singing*]

… that saved a wretch like me…

SANDY: And all these big tough guys would have tears running down their faces and I'd be crying too, trying not to let my bloody mascara run.

[*Singing*] ... I once was lost but now I'm found
Was blind but now I see.

They stand in contemplation of the horror for a few seconds, then flick the zippos off.

MARGARET: He sent me souvenirs. Fans, Thai silk, a photo of a Christmas party in Vung Tau where a young conscript mate of his had 'Draught beer, not boys' written on his back. He wrote about concerts where girls in pink feathers sang 'My Boomerang Won't Come Back' and how his platoon were building a playground for orphans near his base. He said, 'Don't worry about me, love, the only danger I'm in is the possibility of being hit by a flying beer can'.

SCENE FOUR: A WORKADAY WAR

RUTH: Dong Koi was packed every night with soldiers drinking away their fear. I met a young bloke from Sydney in the Dreamland Bar. We got pissed together. He told me that morning his unit had captured some Viet Cong and he'd radioed back to his base for instructions. 'How many prisoners?' came the reply. 'Seven', he said. 'How many did you say?' 'Seven, sir.' 'How many?' came the reply again, until it dawned on him what the base wanted to hear. 'None, sir.' Then they shot all seven Viet Cong. We drank till dawn. And as he staggered off he said, 'How can I tell this to my wife?'.

MARGARET: There were Tupperware parties and card nights with the other army wives. We lived in dread of the staff cars that would arrive in our street, when an officer would come to tell one of us that a husband had been injured, killed or was missing in action. I was sitting in the front room, writing James a letter, when I saw one of those cars stop outside my house. I froze in terror as the man came up the pathway and rang the bell. Trembling, I opened the door and he said, 'Oh, hello, I'm here to do a house inspection, would you be available?'. And then the letters stopped. And after, they started again, but now he wrote of the Battle of Coral, of the explosions, the shellfire, the rat-tat-tat of the guns, mines that would blow up someone to pieces in front of his eyes, young soldiers of twenty, twenty-one, who had been absolutely castrated, of his mates who died next to him, and one in his arms. He was repatriated and when they brought him home, a ghost of the boy I'd waved goodbye, the bloke who delivered him said, 'Well, Mrs, you'll have to look after him now'.

SANDY: The boys were lost souls. So to have someone say, 'It's okay, I'm with you', to listen to them, have some laughs, a few drinks, really helped them for a little while, in that bloody wilderness. When people think of entertainers in Vietnam, they think Bob Hope. Well, I'm here to tell you that Bob never even spent a night in Vietnam. He'd fly in, do his show and then retreat to the Hilton in Bangkok. *We'd* sleep on the cement at the airport waiting for a lift out to Da Nang or Pleiku or wherever to do our show. But we were last on the list, at the end of the food chain. Pigs or chooks or *anything* breathing would have first priority. We'd be carting four suitcases. One for shoes, one for underwear and wigs, and the other two had show gowns. All drip-dry, because we didn't think they'd have many dry cleaners in Vietnam. The false eyelashes, the fishnet stockings and the platinum blonde wigs! Which was bizarre. There, in the red dust of Vietnam, you had to be blonde.

KATHY: Even in that bloody heat we'd wear our bloody uniform. You had to look the part for our boys to come in and say we're home, we're right, someone's looking after us. We'd wear stockings, the stiff white veil and just a splash of 4711. There are three sexes, aren't there? Men, women and nurses. A boy I was looking after complained to me that he hadn't seen a woman in three months!

MARGARET: When James'd get home from work, he'd want me showered, made up, my hair done, always a skirt, slacks were not allowed. He said he liked to admire me. But he'd say, 'You look lovely', and make it sound like a threat. But if I wasn't immaculate, he'd abuse me. It was like walking on eggshells. I always had to act the role of the perfect, happy housewife. He started to talk in his sleep. His eyes would be open but he'd be asleep. His eyes would change, they'd be full of anger, hate, fear. He'd say, 'Get your rifle ready', or 'Watch those trees'. Every night would be like being in Vietnam. He'd relive the most horrendous experiences, with me frozen stiff in the bed beside him. One night he suddenly woke up. I told him what he'd been saying. He looked at me and whispered, 'You ever tell anyone, I'll kill you'.

EVE: Distant bombs rattled my windows at night and flares lit up the sky. Saigon was being hit by hundreds of rockets. I'd hear the first one coming, grab my pillow and roll under the bed. I knew God would protect me, but I wasn't averse to a bit of technological back-up, like the American plane they called 'Puff the Magic Dragon'. When it flew over, the Viet Cong stopped shelling and I could get back into bed. In the mornings, on my way to work, helicopters flew so low you could almost touch them. Camping outside my house, in tin huts, were South Vietnamese soldiers who'd been discarded, limbless, half their faces were missing, and I'd arrive at the orphanage, see row upon row of children in their cots, crying, staring into space or banging their heads against the metal bars. I'd start mixing up the porridge, handing out the hugs and getting the children singing, 'Jesus loves me, this I know, for the Bible tells me so'. And at night, as I tried to sleep, sometimes I'd imagine myself as Ingrid Bergman as the Christian missionary in that film *The Inn of the Sixth Happiness*, and I'd be leading the orphans over the mountains to safety, as they sang, 'Knick knack paddy whack, give a dog a bone, this old man came…'

She breaks down, losing her composure.

MARGARET: We went to the RSL club for a night out. And the bloke at the door asked him if he was a member. And he said, 'No, but I've just come back from 'Nam'. And the doorman said, 'Oh, have you just? Well, come back, sonny, when you've fought a real war.' And James just exploded. I had to drag him off the guy. We went to a dinner party, all prawn cocktails and beef stroganoff, and this young woman, a uni type, peace badges and cheesecloth, started in on him, going on about how wrong the war was, and didn't he feel ashamed, blah blah blah. And he started to get very upset. Very. But she would not stop, so I took her out to the kitchen and, over a glass of Blue Nun, I said, 'Listen, love, you don't know what the fuck you're talking about, excuse my French, but you weren't there. I'd be very careful if I were you because he's got bloody war neurosis and, unless you shut up, he might just reach over and punch your smug little face right out.' I quite enjoyed that. If I hadn't had my sense of humour, I would have been walking round wearing one of those canvas blazers with wrap-around sleeves. Instead I'd get stuck into the wine, a smiling depressive, and be the life of the party.

KATHY: There was a young soldier who'd been at the Battle of Long Tan. His hands were heavily bandaged and he asked me to write a letter to his wife. 'My darling, you asked what I'd like to eat on my first day home. Definitely not fish, rice or beans. I've had enough of them to last me a bloody lifetime.

KATHY *goes to the 'bar'. During the following speech, she pours tea and gives the others a cup each.*

'For breakfast, I'd like ice-cold milk and Rice Bubbles, scrambled eggs, crisp bacon, toast with marmalade and hot, sweet tea. Lunch: toasted tomato sandwich or cheese and lettuce with thin bread and butter cut into triangles. Iced coffee. Dinner: pea soup. Roast mutton, peas, mashed potato. Canned peaches, ice-cold with cream. We'll have milk coffee in the sitting room. Can you get me a bottle of McWilliam's Cream Sherry from the self-serve, also a little bottle of Beenleigh Rum and some ice blocks from the fridge. We can sit in the cool and clean and quiet and toast each other's health and future.'

MARGARET: Every time he went out drinking, I held my breath. I'd have liked to be a hundred miles away when he walked through the front door, drunk and crazy. Once, he literally did walk through the door. I said, 'Do you want your tea?', and he said, 'No, I don't want it, fuck ya!', and off he went straight through the door, straight through the glass door and the screen door. He couldn't feel anything. When he had these attacks, he'd have the strength of ten men. I was there to honour and obey. If his socks were around the wrong way in the drawer he'd let me know. A baked dinner every Monday, if I tried to vary the routine there would be a scene. If we had bills to pay, I'd hide them or he'd fly into a rage. I had a girlfriend over once and he came home from the pub. He put his arms around her. I could see she was embarrassed. I said, 'Don't do that, love', and he picked up a kitchen knife and threw it at me. And I went and found a band-aid then poured us all a beer and we acted like nothing had happened. I still have the scar.

SANDY: There were so many soldiers at Da Nang, it was like a small American city. Cinemas, baseball parks, jogging tracks, bowling alleys, bars and brothels. I'd see this young girl staring out the window of one of the brothels. She was about my age, sometimes she'd wave to me and I'd wave back. One day she motioned me over to her window. Through the bars she handed me a piece of paper and then she was gone. I had the message translated and it read 'Please help me to get out of here'. I talked an Aussie conscript guy into going to the brothel and conning the madam into believing he was a customer and wanted that girl. I waited outside her window. He got her into the room, somehow kicked the window out and helped the girl out to me. I was shit scared. The three of us drove away quickly in his Chevy before old Madam Fang got on our trail. You know, that girl eventually married a GI. She's got three kids, lives in Tucson, Arizona, and every year she sends me a Christmas card.

KATHY: If we had our veils on, the boys saluted us and we could just stand to attention, which was nice. But if we had our jungle greens on and our army hat, we were supposed to salute back. If I'd see the boys coming, I'd whip my hat off and then I didn't have to salute back. I was considered to be too friendly with everybody, I could barely tell the difference between officers and other ranks. I'd get into trouble for calling them 'love' or 'dear'. Sometimes we'd work thirty-six hours straight, we behaved like drunks we were so bloody exhausted. I think I finally realised I wasn't at home anymore when one of the doctors had succumbed to stress (and who could bloody blame him?) and got really drunk the night before an amputation. He was appallingly hungover and said, 'Nurse, I'll have to talk you through it, while you wield the saw. Do you think you can manage that?'. I took a deep breath and automatically said, 'Of course I can, dear'.

RUTH: Seventy percent of my time was spent waiting for something to happen. I was invited to lavish parties thrown by well-heeled Vietnamese. The men with their polished hair, the ladies with theirs lacquered, if they fell down on the streets, they'd crack the bloody concrete, and a few token westerners. Which, being big-titted, round-eyed and blond, meant I was often on the invite list. As long as I left my notebook at home, I was fine. I didn't need notes to remember the obscene opulence of those gatherings, held in mansions set among slums hammered together from discarded Coke cans. I saw richness where you ate off gold dishes, I saw people who fed their children gruel and others who fed paté to their dogs. Lobster had been flown in, waiters came round with wine, martinis, champagne, and there were people across the street who didn't have enough to fill their rice bowls. And, quite frankly, I didn't even take a doggy bag over to them. Over the tinkly cocktail music you could hear flares dropping and guns firing, and I thought, 'I could be dead tomorrow, why shouldn't I enjoy this?'.

SCENE FIVE: CHILDREN

We hear angelic boy sopranos in a cathedral.

KATHY: Whenever I could, I'd get a lift into Saigon for Mass at Nôtre Dame Cathedral. I'd do the Stations of the Cross, whispering my prayers with the rosary beads my dad gave me. Outside on Lam Son Square is a towering statue of the Virgin Mary. In the shade of the statue there would always be a young boy selling lottery tickets. He was on a type of wooden trolley. He had no legs. They'd been blown off by a landmine and his family had deserted him. I asked him how I could help. He said, 'If you want to help me, give me medicine to die'.

SANDY: The very first bombing I ever saw, it was like a movie. It wasn't real. I'd been smoking grass with a soldier from Sydney and suddenly realised it was past curfew. I kissed him goodnight and was trying to creep home through the dark streets. I remember I passed a temple and the smell of incense was strong. Then tracers were going down and there was a little boy walking towards me. And I shouted, 'Hurry hurry!'. He started to run towards me. There were more tracers. And then he just blew up and disappeared in the smoke and fire.

EVE: I was in my old Renault, on my way to collect the corpse of a little boy for burial. I picked his ruined little body up from the morgue. It was wrapped in newspaper and a string bag. And I popped him in the boot of my car. I was caught in a bad traffic jam on Le Loi. I thought, 'How is this happening that I'm driving round Saigon with this little boy's body in my boot and no one would think anything peculiar of it?'.

RUTH: Marilyn was an American army nurse I'd meet for a drink now and then. She was always jotting things down in her journal. One day she seemed a bit down and I said, 'Don't worry, this will all be over soon. You'll be back in California—a white, picket fence and triplets!'. She said it was unlikely she'd choose to have children, she was convinced the sprays they were using could affect a pregnancy. She opened her journal and showed me what she had written:

I choose not to know
If my eggs are misshapen and withered
As the trees by the river,
If snipers are hidden
In the coils of my DNA.

MARGARET: When I was pregnant with James junior we painted the spare room all white. And he built a cradle out in the garage, he'd be out there every night, working on it till it was perfect. He was mostly sweet. Just sometimes, I'd never know whether I'd get a kiss or a punch. But when he'd finally finished and brought it proudly into the baby's room, and I'd put up the pretty mobiles and the pictures of Mickey Mouse and Tinkerbell, we looked at each other, over that cradle, and hoped we could put Vietnam behind us, and that our baby would be welcomed by a happy, normal mum and dad. Like we'd imagined as we'd walked along Five Mile Beach.

She walks out into the rice paddy stage left.

KATHY: I talked to that boy every time I went to Nôtre Dame. I unofficially adopted him. It took a long time to gain his trust. I prayed for him and with the help of some good Aussie soldiers we raised some money and we flew him to Australia where he was fitted with the latest artificial limbs. He learned to walk again and returned to Saigon.

EVE: We piled over two hundred of our children onto a dilapidated American military plane. It was the only flight available out of this hell-hole; en route to their foster homes. My Sydney colleagues, Marie and Leonie, were among the children's escorts. I was due to go with them, but decided to stay for the next airlift. I stood by the staircase as the children boarded the plane in single file, the smaller ones in the arms of the escorts. Leonie was last on, a child holding each of her hands. She got to the top of the stairs and turned to me and said, 'Look who's Ingrid Bergman now! See you soon, love.' I waved the plane goodbye, standing on that tarmac. It seemed to only be in the air for a minute before it plummeted to the ground. All my friends were killed and seventy-eight of the children. Sometimes it felt like it was hard to believe in my god in Vietnam.

'ONE TIN SOLDIER' (Joni Mitchell)

EVE: [*singing*]

Listen children to a story that was written long ago
'Bout a kingdom on a mountain and the valley folk below
On the mountain was a treasure buried deep beneath a stone
And the valley people swore they'd have it for their very own

ALL: [*together, singing*]

Go ahead and hate your neighbour
Go ahead and cheat a friend
Do it in the name of Heaven
Justify it in the end
There won't be any trumpets blowing
Come the judgement day
On the bloody morning after
One tin soldier rides away

EVE: [*singing*]

So the people of the valley sent a message up the hill
Asking for the buried treasure, tons of gold for which they'd kill
Came an answer from the mountain 'with our brothers we will share
All the secrets of our mountain, all the riches buried there'

ALL: [*together, singing*]

Go ahead and hate your neighbour
Go ahead and cheat a friend
Do it in the name of Heaven
Justify it in the end
There won't be any trumpets blowing
Come the judgement day

On the bloody morning after
One tin soldier rides away

EVE: [*singing*]

Now the valley cried with anger, 'Mount your horses, draw your swords'
And they killed the mountain people, so they won their just reward
Now they stood beside the treasure, on the mountain dark and red
Turned the stone and looked beneath it
'Peace on Earth' was all it said

ALL: [*together, singing*]

Go ahead and hate your neighbour
Go ahead and cheat a friend
Do it in the name of Heaven
Justify it in the end
There won't be any trumpets blowing
Come the judgement day
On the bloody morning after
One tin soldier rides away

EVE: [*singing*]

On the bloody morning after
One tin soldier rides away.

SCENE SIX: HUMAN BEINGS

RUTH: [*typing as she speaks*] Most of my 'colleagues' treated me as the greatest laughing stock of all time because I was a woman, and how dare I be in Saigon on their territory? 'She's got her periods, she can't do it, she's only here for one thing.' And the wire agency only wanted to know how 'Joe Bloggs from Minneapolis' felt. 'Hi, Mom, had a great Christmas, got your presents.' They did not encourage any deeper analysis, sometimes I felt I was back on the bloody 'Women's Pages'. Although they liked a bit of action, a touch of 'bang-bang, let's hear the noise, see the blood'. But depicting the Vietnamese as human beings was the last thing they wanted to know.

A new musical theme starts. SANDY, EVE *and* KATHY *appear in the rice paddy stage right.*

SANDY: I'll tell you about an old lady.

SANDY *flicks open a fan which has the face of the 'old lady' on it.*

She was about two hundred years old, very bent, silver hair in a knot and she was crying. She was at the transport depot trying to get a ticket on the same plane we were going on, to get up-country for a show. But no one would give her a ticket. I started to talk to her and she said her son had been found dead in a marsh with a lot of other soldiers and she wanted to go to see his body…

EVE: At times God poked me in the back. Like the day at Ban Me Thuot when I stumbled on the interrogation of an old Vietnamese man.

EVE *flicks open a fan which has the face of the 'old Vietnamese man' on it.*

There was an immense GI with an M16 trained on the old man. He had a scraggy, long beard and a very patrician face. He was kneeling and they were about to put a sandbag over his head…

KATHY: It was one of the first days we'd had an 'outing' from the hospital. There was this lady in a paddy field.

KATHY *flicks open a fan which has the face of 'the lady' on it.*

And she's digging a hole in the ground and these other ladies are getting bits of grass and lining this hole…

SANDY: So I stood on my hind legs and screeched and screamed and got her a ticket. And I bodily lifted this old woman onto that plane…

EVE: And he looked at me straight in the eye…

SANDY: And we arrived at Hue and she would not let go of my hand. Lined up were about a hundred bodies with their hands tied behind their backs. They had all been shot in the back of the neck…

KATHY: And suddenly this little lady squatted over this hole and started to groan. She made these little sounds, a couple of grunts and then there was this tiny baby…

SANDY: The bodies were decomposing but she found her son. I asked her how did she know it was him and she said it was because he had a bent little finger. And she held onto my hand and she cried and cried. I'll never forget that old lady. She told me that I should leave Vietnam soon because God had found an excuse not to be there.

EVE: It wasn't for pity and it wasn't resignation. He was proud and I looked at him and felt such despair, and the old man said to the GI, 'The crimes that you have committed here are greater than the rivers and mountains and deeper than the oceans', and the hood went over his head. I said, 'Why are you doing this?'. The GI said, 'Ma'am, he's a suspected Viet Cong informer'. I said, 'Well, so could I be'. He said, 'Hardly likely, ma'am, you're not a Gook'.

KATHY: It was the most magical thing. We took her and her baby in the chopper to Da Nang. That would be the highlight of my life, to see that woman when her child was born. There was something about seeing that woman, who's the giver of all, giving back to the earth what she's taken from it. She's put another life on that red earth to carry on from herself.

SCENE SEVEN: R & R—ROMANCE & RAPE

The 'Romance' theme starts. The lanterns glow.

RUTH: [*typing as she speaks*] The men would get to escape to Bangkok or Manila or Kings Cross for R & R, Rest and Recreation. But I started to see that the women in Vietnam had their own R & R: but theirs was Romance and Rape.

KATHY: The army mechanics in Vung Tau donated an old, pink Citroen to the nurses. It had no reverse gear but you could drive it if you had a wide enough circle to turn in. That beautiful, pink car was the best thing that happened to us. Because there wasn't anywhere to go if you had a boyfriend and wanted a bit of a cuddle. So you'd drive that Citroen to China Beach, left-hand drive, with your soldier boy beside you. But if you're asking did this convent-bred girl sleep with them… no, ma'am!

SANDY: Oh, bullshit.

KATHY: But when I think of romance, what instantly comes to mind is that old, French, pink car on a barbed-wire beach in Vietnam.

SANDY: I was at Da Nang Airport when it came under attack. I was with a GI named Scotty. A rocket went off and he threw me to the ground. He said if we laid in this bomb crater, it'd be really unlikely another rocket would hit the same place because they don't waste the ammunition, they move the gun slightly on. That was the best chat-up line I've ever heard. So we lay in that crater for an hour or so, in each other's arms, watching it all go across the sky above us. It was incredible, amazing. We didn't make love or anything…

KATHY: Bullshit!

SANDY: … but it was the most romantic experience of my life.

EVE: I'd visit soldiers in the hospitals to see what I could do to help. I'd sit and listen and get their torment about their sexual problems. You know, how their wives were probably having it.

MARGARET: Bullshit!

EVE: And how they weren't, or if they were they were having it with a slope, not a round-eye. I was torn between guilt at not being sympathetic and disgust at the attitudes of some of them. I was propositioned at least six times a day and this, combined with seeing all these guys in their pyjamas raving on about their sex life, or lack of it, nearly put me off men altogether.

ALL: Oh, bullshit!

The women stand on their chairs, looking out into the distance.

KATHY: I was up on the rooftop terrace of the Majestic Hotel, looking out over the Saigon River. The US Embassy were giving the reception. I was dancing with a GI and he asked me if I wanted to go to a real party. I said yes and fifteen minutes later, we were passing over the Majestic in a bloody chopper and I gave them all a wave. On the way the helicopter came under attack, but we arrived at the party in Vung Tau as scheduled. He told me not to talk about the attack because if anyone in command knew, they'd cancel the airlifts to the parties.

SANDY: Out on the terrace, up on the roof of the Majestic Hotel, a mariachi band played, as I was waving back to some girl overhead in a chopper. There was a guy from the British Embassy next to me, and while he was trying to cop a feel he was giving us a rather old-fashioned lecture. He said he could get us all guns, so if the Viet Cong ever took over the city, we could shoot ourselves rather than be raped. We said we'd take our chances, thanks, Charles.

RUTH: There was a party at the Majestic and I was chatting to the most darling Asian man, a Vietnamese-Chinese, a short guy with a smile from ear to ear, the sweetest man you've ever met in your life. A gentlemen of the highest quality, he'd open your car door, hold your chair out, pour your champagne. He went to the bar to get me another drink and a journo whispered to me that this charming guy's claim to glory was that he could interrogate somebody, break every bone in their body and not leave a single bruise. And I looked up and saw him coming back with my champagne and flashing me that smile. And I walked straight past him and out to the lift.

EVE: I was on my way up in the lift to the terrace of the Majestic Hotel. It had been a day when I could not go to the orphanage and face the mosquitos, the sweat, the heat. So I had a siesta. In the afternoon I had my hair done and walked through the sandbagged streets in my best Thai silk. I stepped out of the lift to the terrace and a short man, a Vietnamese, with a charming smile, handed me a champagne. And we looked over the river at the war on the horizon. The whole time there was this distant boom boom boom, which we could hear even as the mariachi band played on. And for once I just enjoyed this man's company and tried not to think that each of those boom boom booms was probably killing someone. It was my twenty-second birthday.

MARGARET: It was his birthday and I thought I'd cook him a nice dinner, make it like a little party. Half past six and he's not home. Quarter to ten, he walks in. He's got this birthday cake that says 'Happy Twenty-First Birthday, James'. I said, 'Oh, that's a nice cake, James', but didn't say anything about the twenty-first, he was actually twenty-nine now. He said, 'We're having a party and you're not invited'. And he sits our little son up at the table. He's got this dirty great knife to cut it with, matches in the cake, no candles, and he's singing 'Happy Twenty-First Birthday' to me and glasses and plates are smashed to the floor. Then I managed to put the boy to bed and I went down to my girlfriend's house for a while. When I came back, he was out cold on the couch, I could see him from the porch light shining through the venetians. He had a huge ghurka's knife next to him. I put my hand on the light switch, it was taped over. I went through the house and every switch had been taped over so he could wait for me in the darkness. I wasn't his wife anymore, I was the enemy. I went into my son's room and locked the door.

RUTH: I was in love with this wonderful man. He was a Green Beret, tall, strong, tanned and handsome. He told me we'd go to live in New York City when it was all over. He went out on an operation and I waited, up on the Rex Hotel terrace, watching the war in the distance. And I waited two days and then I knew he was dead. I insisted on seeing his body. He was swollen like a water buffalo, his skin was all black and cracked. I still wear the Star of David I cut from his neck.

EVE: As much as I thought about marriage, I thought about marrying a Vietnamese man. Mr Tran was the driver and handyman at the orphanage. Gradually, we began to meet on Sundays, a walk to a temple, a stroll through the markets... We started to become very close. He began to tell me the teachings of his religion, Confucianism. Walking through Giac Lam Pagoda he explained that Confucian thinking demanded that the woman's position be inferior to the man's; that she defer to him like a 'little sister'. I think it was his subtle way of telling me our cultures were never going to meet. We continued to work together, but on Sundays after that, I strolled alone.

MARGARET *walks amongst the others as they hover over her, standing on their chairs, like protecting angels.*

MARGARET: He was on a raid and he'd come to get me, and he shot his rifle and it hit the plaster. My son was hiding in the next room. And he put the rifle under his jacket and we drove down to the beach. His face was changing. His eyes. And we went and sat by the water and he put the gun in his mouth. He said, 'How would it be if I blew your brains out and then blew mine out too?'. But then we drove back home. He said, 'Don't worry, we're going to bed'. I said, 'I'm not going to bed with you'. But he grabbed me, held me at gunpoint and said, 'Get undressed and get into bed'. And I did. He had the gun pointed at me. He pushed me against the wall and had sex with me. He blacked out after that. I'm laying there with him against me with the gun under my chin. And I heard a car pull up. My son had called the police. And he gave himself up to the police very calmly. I charged him with it all, including rape, but they just included that as assault, as I was his wife. He was sentenced to five years and it took me those five years till I could find a way out of it all.

'WILL YOU STILL LOVE ME TOMORROW' (Carole King)

RUTH: [*singing*]

Tonight you're mine completely
You give your love so sweetly
Tonight the light of love is in your eyes
But will you love me tomorrow

MARGARET: [*singing*]

Is this a lasting treasure
Or just a moment's pleasure
Can I believe the magic of your sighs
Will you still love me tomorrow

RUTH & MARGARET: [*together, singing*]

Tonight with words unspoken
You said that I'm the only one
But will my heart be broken
When the night

ALL: [*together, singing*]

When the night

RUTH: [*singing*]

Meets the morning

ALL: [*together, singing*]

Meets the morning sun…

SANDY: I was wanted, admired, appreciated, adored! The dangers of this euphoria were really second to the wonderful times. That's why I stayed so long, we were like diamonds in the dirt…

SANDY, EVE *and* KATHY *become a slow-motion, Motown-style girl group, with* SANDY *singing lead, as we hear 'And here they are, boys, live in Da Nang tonight, the fabulous Velveteens!'. Applause and whistles. As they sing, rockets explode, people scream and tracers shoot through the sky.*

MARGARET *and* RUTH *sit in their chairs, watching the show, locked in their memories.*

SANDY, EVE & KATHY: [*together, singing*]

Tonight with words unspoken
You said that I'm the only one

But will my heart be broken
When the night (when the night)
Meets the morning (meets the morning) sun
I'd like to know that your love
Is love I can be sure of
So tell me now and I won't ask again…

RUTH *and* MARGARET *join the ghostly singing group.*

ALL: [*together, singing*]
Will you still love me tomorrow
Will you still love me tomorrow
Will you still love me tomorrow?

SCENE EIGHT: WAR DOES BECOME NORMAL

The women sit on the terrace. A starry night.

KATHY: The Vietnamese used to sit on the steps outside the surgical suite and chatter away. One day they were suddenly quiet. So I went outside and coming towards me were six gentlemen in black pyjamas with bandoliers of bullets across their chests and one hand holding machine guns and the other holding a stretcher which they dropped in front of me. And there was a bloodied Viet Cong man. No one had 'I'm a friend' or 'I'm a foe' tattooed on their forehead. I never thought you could say, 'We're not going to heal you because you are the enemy'. They were human beings, they were hurting. When the prisoners were taken from the hospital, all the drips and plasters we'd used to help them live would be ripped out. I once spent hours doing a complicated amputation on a Viet Cong guy and I trimmed it off really nicely. A week later I heard that he was shot and hanged. I was bloody pissed off.

EVE: I was on my way to a remote airstrip to see off a sergeant whose tour of duty was up. He was going home. He was a bit plastered after goodbye drinks with his mates. He saw something going on in a field and jumped out. He should have stayed in that bloody jeep. He had no right to do this. He ran in, there was a big explosion and I did the most stupid thing of my life. I ran in after him. His legs were blown off. There was not a thing I could do but pray. I cradled what was left of his body. I cuddled him. He thought I was his wife who he was going home to be with. For the rest of his life. He spoke to me, told me how wonderful it was to be in my arms again. How much he loved me. I told him I loved him too and what we and the kids were going to do the next weekend. I played the role of his wife and it took fifteen minutes for him to die in my arms. About a year later I went to see Brian's wife at home and told her about his last moments. She cried. She said, 'These are the first tears of joy I've had since then, knowing that he died with someone who loved him'. And I said, 'No'. She said, 'Yes; because you were me.'

RUTH: I went and watched an interrogation. They had a young girl who looked about fifteen. And they had one of her legs in a bucket of water and one in another. She was naked and they had a car battery and wires attached to her. They'd ask her a question and whatever answer she gave they'd give her a jolt. She didn't know I was there. She was in such a state of shock. Her eyes were closed. They said she was Viet Cong. And this was all conducted by Vietnamese, it wasn't the bloody Yanks. I think they wanted to shock me, but I wouldn't let them see that I was. I went back to my hotel room and I started to shake and shake. I can still hear that little girl screaming to this day. But I refused to be shocked in front of those bastards.

EVE: I also saw GIs who were equally proud of their victims. A young soldier came out of one of the brothels and bumped into me as I passed by. He said, 'Sorry, ma'am', and walked on through the crowd. I saw that he'd dropped his wallet and picked it up. It fell open. There were two photos inside. One of him with his family, another of him, smiling, holding the severed head of a Viet Cong soldier. Suddenly he was back beside me, 'Thanks, ma'am', grabs the wallet, disappears. I sometimes wonder if that photograph made it into his family album and what he thinks of himself.

SANDY: I think something happens to you in a war zone which is completely different to the way you are at home having fish and chips. I loved it. I loved the fear and the action. The challenge. I enjoyed the people, the markets, even the stench. It's a game of survival. We were travelling one night from Qui Nhon on the coast to An Kae up in the hills. There was only a truck and a jeep available. But they were minus a rear gunner. I volunteered and I'm sitting there like Rambo with this M16, they're magnificent guns, so accurate, no recoil. I learnt to use one while I was hanging round the bases between shows. We'd go to the riverbank and shoot cans. Fabulous. So it was a black night and we wound our way up these hills, up these high mountains, and I swear if anything or anyone had moved in those bushes I would have killed it and not thought about it for a split second. I felt then that feeling of survival that you don't ever feel in suburbia.

MARGARET: It was bloody degrading to have to go to Social Security and say, 'My son and I are desperate. My husband's a psycho 'cause he went to Vietnam.' The men have got their pension, their medical assistance. I served in the army too. There should be a hotline where I can say, 'Help me, please'. Christ, it was a battle. I was very low at one point, thought I was on the verge of suicide, when the Salvation Army put me onto Linkline, which was run by the wives of Vets. They listened to me in my darkest moments and it was somehow comforting to realise there were other women like me, I thought I was the only one. I started to write to James in jail. He asked me to donate his uniform, of which he was very proud, to the Vietnam Vet's Association. When I went there and started to meet other Vets, it was oddly therapeutic. I decided to do something to help these blokes before they ended up like my husband. So I took myself off to school and I became a counsellor, which I am to this day. And a loudmouth who speaks up for their rights when they can't do it themselves. An American soldier wrote: 'I died in Vietnam, I just didn't know it'. And my James and so many other Australian blokes did too.

We hear Bing Crosby singing 'I'm Dreaming of a White Christmas' through a crackly speaker. The women begin to pack their bags. A siren starts to wail.

SCENE NINE: GOODNIGHT SAIGON

One by one, they group together downstage. A helicopter sound is heard along with the score.

RUTH: And we were told that we'd know that Saigon was about to fall, that the North Vietnamese were about to enter the city, when the

Voice of America would broadcast: 'It is one hundred and twelve degrees and rising', followed by Bing Crosby singing 'White Christmas'. That was the signal to evacuate, to go to one of the helipad sites to fly out of Vietnam.

EVE: In those last days, when the Americans thundered past in their army vehicles, they seemed like a space fiction image to me. You'd see these huge young men who were very tall and muscular, bronzed and golden-haired, standing on these machines. I'd become so close to the Vietnamese, I was physically repelled by people of non-Asian appearance. I ran across a missionary family one day and was struck by their little, blonde, pasty-faced children with their pale eyes. Afterwards I said to my Vietnamese friend, Miss Lei, 'Oh dear, aren't they ugly?', and she said, 'Eve, don't you ever look in the mirror these days?'. It was time to go home...

RUTH: And as I flew out, on my way to Bangkok and then home, I thought of the bar girls at the Nautique, the 'five o'clock follies' on the roof of the Rex Hotel where the US image-makers told their lies and the love I'd said goodbye to in a Saigon morgue...

SANDY: We arrived at the airport and I gave my last few dollars to some kids who looked like they needed a feed. I managed to get a call through to our booking agent in Sydney. His secretary answered and told me that the bastard had pissed off with all our money from this last year in Vietnam. You had to laugh.

KATHY: On the last day, I accompanied injured troops back home. There were rows of coffins on board. A young soldier who was coming home with us came up to me and pointed at a coffin. 'Look after that one, Sister, that's my brother in there'...

RUTH: We flew over a rubber plantation. The trees were all planted in steadfast rows, like soldiers. And I remembered being there, looking at it, and an old Vietnamese man who'd said, 'Come with me, madam, and I'll show you the tiger'. And I said, 'Oh, bullshit!'. I'd had a few drinks by then. But at six o'clock the next morning, rap rap rap on my door, and I got up...

EVE: As the helicopter took off from the roof of the US Embassy I saw Vietnamese men, women and children clamouring at the gates desperate to escape before the city fell. So many broken promises. I thought of Miss Lei and Mr Tran, I wondered what would happen to them now. I thought of how I had loved their way of relating. They use these beautiful expressions which paint a picture of how they're feeling. The basic word for blue and green is the same, *xanh*, but it's the *xanh* of the sky or the *xnah* of the trees. And as we flew over Saigon for the last time, out of Vietnam, I saw that the blue of their sky was now black and the green of their trees had been stripped bare.

RUTH: Rap, rap, rap. It was a grey dawn and we walked down through the trees and he said, 'There she is!'. And I said, 'Come on, love, you're pulling my chain'. And he said, 'Look, madam, look, she's there!'. And the mist rose in little tendrils and then I saw the slightest movement and there she was. Talk about camouflage! My hair stands on end with absolute rapture just thinking about her. Her eyes are looking at me, golden and clear, and she was a glorious, tawny, black-striped creature. She knew I was there. She looked straight at me and I knew she would be forever in my dreams.

SANDY: I looked out of the window of the plane. My pink feather boa, that must have dropped from my luggage, floated in the hot wind across the tarmac. It made me think of my girlfriend from my first singing group in Vietnam. Years ago, we were in Qui Nhon on the coast. We'd done a show and I was in the tent trying to sleep. She came in crying, looking absolutely in shock. She'd gone walking on the beach, where she shouldn't have been. She'd wanted some peace and quiet, some space. Six GIs had dragged her into a hut, ripped her clothes off and put machine guns to her head. She said they put a German Luger in her mouth. Her spirit went out of her body and she was sitting in that thatched roof, looking down and thinking, 'Oh, that poor girl'. When it was over they discussed whether they should shoot her, but decided not to. She told me all this. I listened, horrified. But then I told her to shut up about it, not to tell anyone, as it would be made to look like it was her fault and maybe we'd be sent home.

KATHY: I looked out of the window and saw a little Vietnamese boy waving to me as the plane taxied away and I remembered the first time I met him. He'd been burnt, napalm, it was as if he'd been dragged along a road and he had skin and tar all mixed up together from his head to his feet. I started at his feet with a bowl of saline and lots of swabs and it took hours. I finally got to his head and he had not made a murmur, not a bloody sound. I wiped the wet swab across his eyelids. He opened his eyes and looked at me. In English, he said, 'Thank you very much'.

MARGARET: And then he was released. I reluctantly agreed to meet him at an Anzac Day March, which was unusual for him. In all the years we'd been together, he'd get dressed for the March, but end up not going, slumped in a chair staring at the wall. So we met, my son would not come. My once-upon-a-time husband thanked me for coming. I re-pinned his medals on straight and watched him march. The only thing he said afterwards was, 'Fuck, it's so bloody sad'. We said goodbye. Some weeks later, he drove to the base where he'd done his training. He gassed himself in his car, right outside the gates. It was over.

SANDY, EVE *and* RUTH *form a funeral tableau.*

MARGARET *takes a small bag, opens it, and begins to pour out her husband's ashes over the rice paddy as* KATHY *sings.*

'SAIGON BRIDE' (Joan Baez/Nina Duscheck)

KATHY: [*singing*]

Farewell my wistful Saigon bride
I'm going out to stem the tide
A tide that never saw the seas
It flows through jungles, round the trees
Some say it's yellow, some say red
It will not matter when we're dead

ALL: [*together, singing*]

How many dead men will it take
To build a dyke that will not break
How many children must we kill
Before we make the waves stand still

KATHY: [*singing*]

Though miracles come high today
We have the wherewithal to pay
It takes them off the street you know
To places they would never go alone
It gives them useful trades
The lucky boys are even paid

ALL: [*together, singing*]

Men die to build their pharaohs' tombs
And still and still the teeming wombs
How many men to conquer Mars
How many dead to reach the stars

KATHY: [*singing*]

Farewell my wistful Saigon bride
I'm going out to stem the tide
A tide that never saw the seas
It flows through jungles, round the trees
Some say it's yellow, some say red
It will not matter when we're dead.

SCENE TEN: AFTERMATH

The bamboo screens upstage open, to reveal an Australian sky.

RUTH: Back in Australia, everything was normal. But it wasn't my normal. My normal was haggle, watch your back, sleep with your jewellery under your pillow, if you hear a bang, hit the dirt. Civilian life was like a desert. 'Bloody hell, it's a fine day, a loaf of bread please, a pint of milk.' There was no excitement, no nothing!

KATHY: I'd change trams in Collins Street to get to the hospital. We'd be in a group, at work, talking everyday normal things, and I'd have to get up and leave because I'd think, 'What the fuck are they talking about that for? That's not worthy of discussion.' The other nurses thought I loved helicopters. I can't see one that I don't think of 'dust-off', the red dust swirling through the air when a helicopter leaves the ground. If I hear one, I have to go to the window and see that chopper flying over the city and the other nurses say, 'Oh, there she goes, she just loves helicopters'. And I just let them laugh, while I flash back, in my mind, in my heart, to my time in the war. When I was there, I learnt to look at my own country in a different way. I learnt what became for me the personal meaning of life. And death. A legacy of the war is the smells associated with it. Grease, oil, perspiration, a smell that khaki has, mould, a jungly smell. If I sniff any of these I'm instantly back in Vietnam. Now I'm ashamed to say that sometimes I don't believe in God. But I do believe in miracles.

SANDY: Just seeing a plastic bag floating on the road would trigger images of the first dead body I saw. That little boy who disappeared into the smoke. But I was back home, in the city, wandering around like an alien, telling myself I was buying some stockings. I heard this strange, rhythmic chanting. It sounded like danger. I lay down in the gutter. Quickly. In the middle of Collins Street, mind you. And then a bunch of Hare Khrishnas danced slowly past, beating their drums.

EVE: I went to the movies at the Regent. Just anything to get away from the way I felt to be home, like a timid tourist in a foreign land. As I walked into that huge, dark place, *MASH* was on the big screen. Helicopters came in with the wounded and the audience started to laugh. And I stood up in the middle of that cinema and a voice came out of me and it shouted, 'Shut up! Stop laughing, you fools! Don't you know this is happening in Vietnam? And it's not funny.' And they all looked at me and I ran out of the darkness into the light and the strange landscape of Collins Street. I felt a stranger in my own home town. When I went to Vietnam I was very narrow-minded. There was only one path, one way, then I saw that life did not fall into neat little bundles. The Vietnamese were really well and truly done over by the French, then the Japanese, then the Brits gave it back to the French, then the American war, thank you very much. I could understand how if I'd been a Vietnamese I probably would have ended up a Communist, fighting for the freedom of what I perceived to be my country.

KATHY: I now work in a Repat Hospital. Often the midnight to dawn shift, and as I walk through the wards, sometimes in the half light, my sleeping boys look to me as they did thirty years ago. When they had their youth and their innocence. Once I came home, I even married a Vet. I had to wake him up with a broom handle, from a distance, for fear he'd go me with the knife he kept under his pillow. After a few years we divorced. And just recently I've married another one. But he's a very nice, gentle, loving man. He has his moments, his flashbacks, but I have a better understanding of it now. I don't cope with 'normal' people, I find them boring. I probably *am* as disturbed as my veterans are, having been with them as long as I have. It's not considered normal or usual to have a dependent husband, but if it works, why not? It works for us, we are mostly happy together. The medals he wears are inscribed with the place of action, the nature of the award and the years 1962 to… There is no cut-off date, as though the war still goes on. I read the other day: 'They say it's over, but how would they know? All the ones that say it, didn't go.'

SANDY: I was only home a couple of months when I decided to escape to Las Vegas. I married a comedian I'd met in Saigon, but eventually the laughs ran out and I came home. Now I live way out in the suburbs and run my own talent school. Teaching kids tap, jazz ballet and singing. I've done quite well and have just started trying to perform again too, entering crappy talent quests in the clubs where I started out. If you were at my place for a few drinks, you'd never know I was in Vietnam. Apart from the little, white statue of Quan Am, the Goddess of Mercy, who sits on my kitchen window sill. Sometimes I can't resist getting out a couple of black and white movies I have of me singing and dancing in Nui Dat. They're getting a bit scratchy now, so I try not to watch them too much.

RUTH: And after a decade of covering the hottest story of the age, of being there in the centre of it, I came home. The only job any of the papers would offer me was a return to the 'Women's Pages'. I told them all they could stick it where it fitted and tore up my press card and walked out. I ended up marrying that bloke who said, 'I dare you!' all those years ago. I look after my husband, do the crosswords, watch the news and drink red wine. Sometimes, late at night, I have a crème de menthe and smoke a Salem, and read my clippings from that war. Long ago, when I was really young. And alive. If I could have saved one child, one family, I would feel a little appeased in my heart. But I didn't. I was stupid. Complacent. I didn't understand and that is a terrible excuse, but I don't think I did. It was disgusting and so very wrong. I hate war now. It's a stinking, revolting man-made way of testing weapons. Women don't declare war. It's men, always men, every President has to have his own bloody war.

EVE: Since I've come back my health has not been good. I somehow started to think it had something to do with the sprays, but they kept saying no. A fellow sprayed every night. He'd walk through these clouds of spray, togged up like something out of Jules Verne. He'd start just before dinnertime and the buildings were just plyboard really, with gaps everywhere. After dinner I'd walk up to the roof for some peace and quiet. Some nights I'd think, 'Oh, it's raining!', but it was just this fine mist coming down on me. But life goes on. If you come to visit me, I live just around the corner from the Vietnamese strip in Richmond. I'll give you a Saigon coffee, with Carnation milk. Delicious. I'll show you the drawings that my sponsor child in Hanoi sends me. Her name is Phuong, which means 'phoenix'. And on my mantelpiece, you'll see a black and white photo of my Vietnamese love, who was not meant to be.

MARGARET: They say I'm a nemesis to the Minister for Veterans' Affairs. Whenever he's speaking at a meeting, I'm there, because I've always got something to put in his hot little hand and say, 'I want action on that, please do something about it'. (Agent Orange being one.) If conscription was ever introduced again, I'd take my son and flee the country or go to prison, anything that would stop my boy turning into his father. And sometimes the nightmares come. They can be doozies. I walk up a never-ending hill with this man. He has no face, but I'm pretty sure it's James . He's holding a rifle. And there are big, black dogs in the dark, with red headbands around their necks. And I wake up in a cold sweat. But I'm bloody determined it's never going to get me down. I'm not getting into that scenario again. Before I so much as go out for the first time with a man, and I mean no offence by this, I require a stat dec that he's never been in Vietnam.

SCENE ELEVEN: EPILOGUE

We hear the military band tuning up again , the noise of the crowd.

SANDY: Oh, I'm not marching. Don't know whether they'd want old show girls like me joining in. But I'll sit up on this pub balcony, have a few champagnes and give them a toast and a wave as they go by. I think all of us who were in Vietnam are part of a special family, bound together by some shared life-altering experience that we'll never ever forget. I mostly talk show business now, Hollywood in the old days, when there was real glamour, but inside there is this other me, the one who wants to talk about that young girl and her adventures in Vietnam.

EVE: I'm not here to march, but as a St John's Ambulance member. I still can't stop volunteering! But I'll wave them on as they pass by. Vietnam is always with me. I was told I must have been Vietnamese in another life which, as a Christian, I don't believe. But now I see myself as part of all countries, all people, all creation and that's what the Vietnam War has given me.

KATHY: When I decided to march today, I finally did something I'd meant to do for years. To get in touch with the family of a young soldier I'd sat with as he died. I searched and searched and finally found his dad. He was very old and I told him that his son hadn't died alone, that I was with him. And that man was so pleased, so relieved that his son didn't die by himself. We put others first in Vietnam, that's what we were trained to do. Sometimes, if they recovered, they wouldn't even recognise us, they would have blocked it out because of the pain. But if they didn't make it, well, that act of helping those soldiers die in that strange country was more intimate than sex, more intimate than childbirth, and once you've done that, you can never be ordinary again.

RUTH: So I'm at the March for the first time, with my journal and camera. After all these years, I've decided I might write again. A novel about a young Australian journalist who went to Vietnam. 'Gee, I'd love to go back to that place, that time.' I've never adjusted and I doubt I ever will. Sometimes I feel I left my soul in Vietnam. I'm going back there next week to see if I can find it.

MARGARET: My son asked me if he could come with me today. So he's marching with his father's unit, wearing his dad's medals for the first time. I always say I waved goodbye to a beautiful, young man and got back a fair mongrel. You never get over it, never. But what I've done is learn to live with it. I hope he's found peace. I nearly put on his headstone: 'The journey has ended, the search is over'. When we were young, in Australia, in our cosy world, could we have ever imagined that a war, in a country far so away, on the South China Sea, would come to change our lives so much? I often have another dream where I fly in a helicopter to that Memorial Wall for the Vietnam Veterans. I look at all the endless names of those who died or disappeared and right at the very end, I look and I look, and then I see my name…

THE CIRCLE GAME (Joni Mitchell)

EVE: [*singing*]

Yesterday a child came out to wonder
Caught a dragon fly inside a jar
Fearful when the sky was full of thunder
And tearful at the falling of a star

SANDY: [*singing*]

Then the child moved ten times round the seasons
Skated over ten clear frozen streams
Words like when you're older must appease him
And promises of someday make his dreams

EVE & SANDY: [*together, singing*]

And the seasons they go round and round
And the painted ponies go up and down
We're captive on the carousel of time
We can't return, we can only look behind
From where we came
And go round and round and round
In the circle game

RUTH: [*singing*]

Sixteen springs and sixteen summers gone now
Cartwheels turn to car wheels through the town
And they tell him
Take your time, it won't be long now
Till you drag your feet to slow the circles down

ALL: [*together, singing*]

And the seasons they go round and round
And the painted ponies go up and down
We're captive on the carousel of time
We can't return, we can only look behind
From where we came
And go round and round and round
In the circle game

KATHY: [*singing*]

So the tears go by and now the boy is twenty
Though his dreams have lost some grandeur coming true

There'll be new dreams, maybe better dreams and plenty
Before the last revolving year is through

ALL: [*together, singing*]

And the seasons they go round and round
And the painted ponies go up and down
We're captive on the carousel of time
We can't return, we can only look behind
From where we came
And go round and round and round
In the circle game

MARGARET: [*singing*]

And go round and round
And round in the circle
Round and round
And round in the circle
Round and round and round
In the circle game.

We hear the military band that we last heard at the beginning of the show.

The cast form a line together and start to march and wave in slow motion. They clutch the battered 'uniforms' that they wore in their Vietnam.

The sound of crowds cheering and clapping.

The women continue to march and wave as they disappear into the darkness.

THE END

For a full list of our titles, visit our website:

www.currency.com.au

Currency Press
The performing arts publisher
PO Box 2287
Strawberry Hills NSW 2012
Australia
enquiries@currency.com.au
Tel: (02) 9319 5877
Fax: (02) 9319 3649